CECIL COUNTY
PUBLIC LIBRARY

JAN 16 2015

301 Newark Ave
Elkton, MD 21921

EDGE BOOKS

U.S. NAVY by the Numbers

by Amie Jane Leavitt

Consultant: Raymond L. Puffer, PhD
Historian, Retired
Edwards Air Force Base History Office

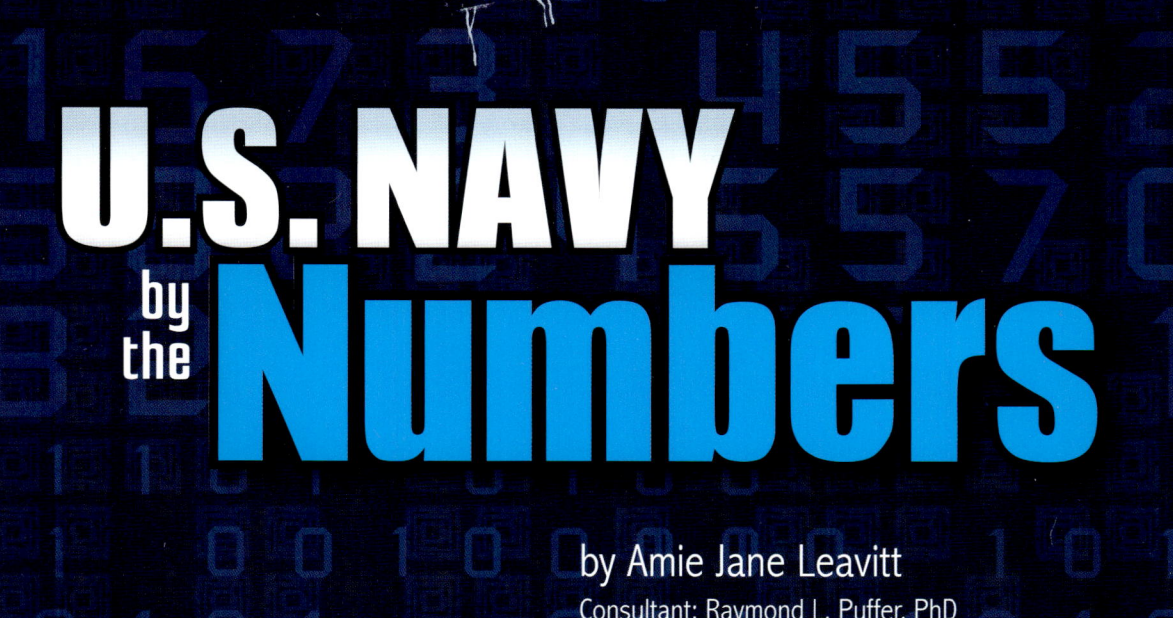

CAPSTONE PRESS
a capstone imprint

Edge Books are published by Capstone Press,
1710 Roe Crest Drive, North Mankato, Minnesota 56003
www.capstonepub.com

Copyright © 2014 by Capstone Press, a Capstone imprint. All rights reserved.
No part of this publication may be reproduced in whole or in part, or stored in a
retrieval system, or transmitted in any form or by any means, electronic, mechanical,
photocopying, recording, or otherwise, without written permission of the publisher.

Library of Congress Cataloging-in-Publication Data
Leavitt, Amie Jane.
U.S. Navy by the numbers / by Amie Jane Leavitt.
    pages cm. — (Edge. Military by the numbers)
 Includes bibliographical references and index.
 Audience: Grades 4 to 6.
 ISBN 978-1-4765-3918-8 (library binding)
 ISBN 978-1-4765-5121-0 (paperback)
 ISBN 978-1-4765-5966-7 (ebook PDF)
1. United States. Navy—Juvenile literature. I. Title.
 VA58.4.L43 2014
 359.00973—dc23   2013035691

Editorial Credits
Mandy Robbins and Brenda Haugen, editors; Heidi Thompson, designer;
Jennifer Walker, production specialist

Photo Credits
Corbis, 24, 25 (Bush); Getty Images: Archive Photos/MPI, 20 (left), Science & Society Picture Library, 20 (right); Naval History & Heritage Command, 26–27; SuperStock: ClassicStock.com, 24, 25 (Congress); U.S. Navy graphic, 6–7; U.S. Navy photo, 24, 25 (VF-44), Lt. Cmdr. Josh Hammond, cover, 1, Lt. Liza Swart, 14, 15, MC1 Cassandra Thompson, 9 (middle), MC1 Curtis K. Biasi, 24, 25 (NASCAR), MC1 James Kimber, 9 (bottom), MC1 James Kimber, 21, MC1 Ricardo Danan, 23, MC1 Tommy Lamkin, 8, MC1 Woody Paschall, 22, MC2 Daniel Barker, 24, 25 (band), MC2 Dominique Pineiro, 25 (refueling), MC2 Ernest R. Scott, 5, MC2 James R. Evans, 13 (both), MC2 James R. Evans, 19, MC2 Jason R. Zalasky, 10 (right, middle), MC2 Jon Dasbach, 9 (top), MC2 Kevin S. O'Brien, 24, 25 (woman), MC2 Marcos T. Hernandez, 24, 25 (raft), MC2 Matthew R. White, 11 (middle), MC2 Zachary L. Borden, 10 (left), MC3 Jonathan Sunderman, 11 (right), MCSN Jared M. King, 12 (top), MCSN John Grandin, 11 (left), MCSN Sabrina Fine, back cover, 18 (right), PH2 Mark A. Ebert, 12 (bottom), PHC John E. Gay, 18 (left), U.S. Navy SEAL and SWCC photo, 24, 25 (SEAL), Wikimedia: US Navy/PH2 William G. Roy/post-work Cobatfor, 28–29

Design Elements
Shutterstock: aarrows, URRRA, Yaraz

* Numbers listed in this title are accurate as of 2013.

Printed in the United States of America in Stevens Point, Wisconsin.
092013   007768WZS14

Table of Contents

World Class Personnel and Fleet............4
Aircraft Carriers: Rulers of the Sea.........6
Aircraft Carrier Strike Group................8
On Land and at Sea......................10
Flying High in the U.S. Navy..............12
Boot Camp! Training Sailors...............14
Becoming a SEAL........................16
Life at Sea..............................18
Into the Deep: Submarines................20
Naval Weapons 22
Counting by 11s.........................24
Attack on Pearl Harbor 26
Midway: A Decisive Battle................28

Glossary................................30
Read More.............................31
Internet Sites...........................31
Index 32

World Class Personnel and Fleet

Members of the United States Navy guard their nation's shores and command the seas. The mobility of their fleet of ships allows them be stationed all over the world. Navy sailors stand ready to deal with enemy threats anywhere at any time.

Personnel in the U.S. Navy
323,225

Active Duty
201,000 civilian employees

11,087 female officers (total active and reserve)

Enlisted
264,766

Officers
53,947

4,512 Midshipmen (sailors in training to become officers)

enlisted—describes a member of the military who is not an officer

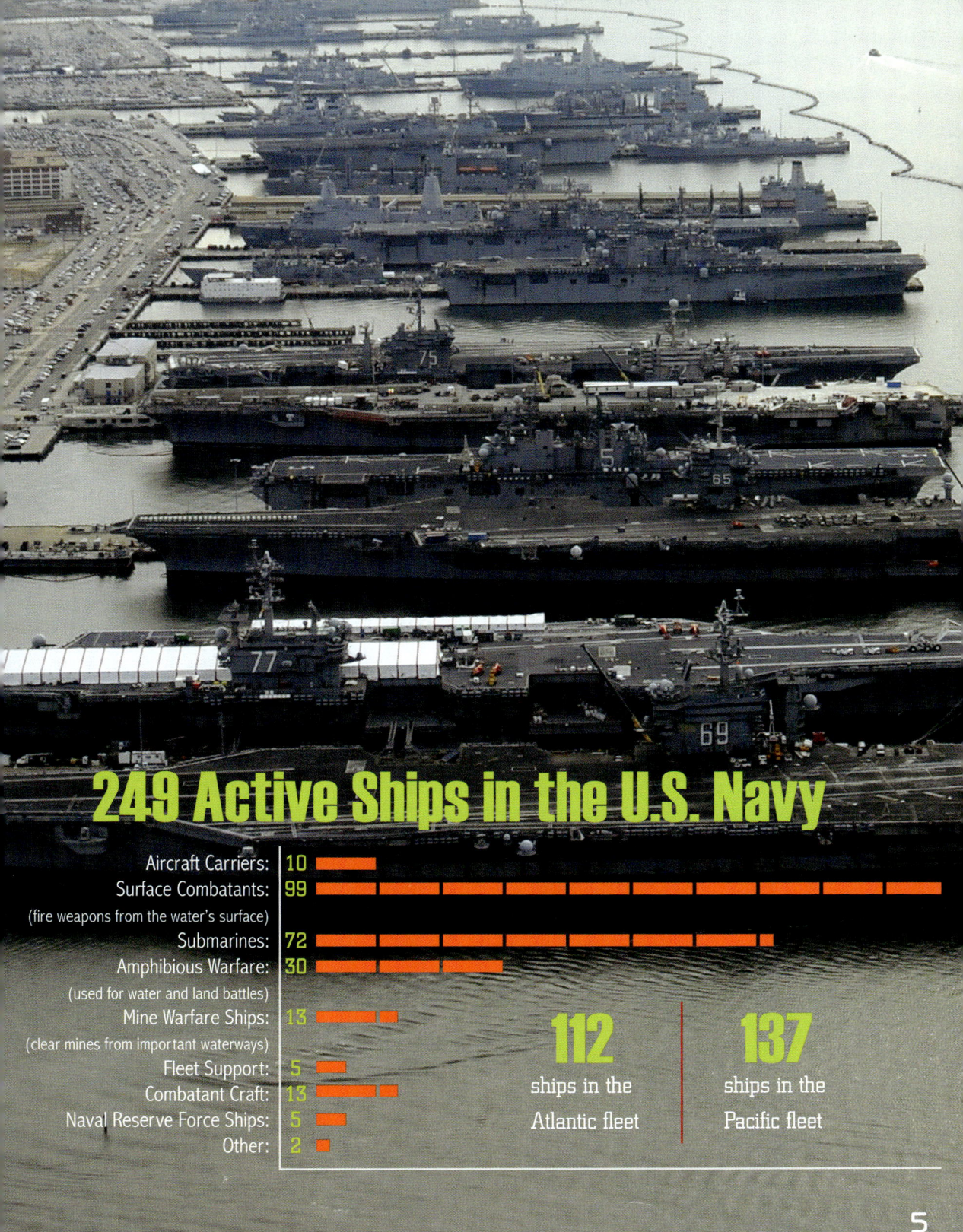

Aircraft Carriers:
Rulers of the Sea

Aircraft carriers are one of the most recognizable U.S. Navy ships. These floating military bases station personnel and aircraft throughout the world. They provide bases for aircraft at sea, allowing for quick air strikes from almost anywhere on the planet.

256 ft. width

The newest class of aircraft carriers is the Gerald R. Ford class. The first ship of this class, the USS *Gerald R. Ford*, will be completed in 2015.

Gerald R. Ford Class Stats

3 deck edge elevators

30+ knots (35 mph): speed

78 1st Gerald R. Ford class aircraft carrier number

4 propellers

4,539 crew members

800 fewer crew members than the previous CVN 68-class ship

50 years: service life

Onboard desalination plants can produce **400,000** gallons of fresh water per day.

up to **90** aircraft on the carrier

10 of this class of ship planned to be built

320 feet: the length given for arresting cables to stop planes traveling at 150 mph

25 years at sea without refueling

1,092 ft.: length = 75-story building lying on its side

stands as tall as a **24-**story building

base—an area run by the military where people serving in the military live and military supplies are stored
knot—an international nautical unit of speed equal to 6,076 feet (1,853 meters) per hour
desalination—the process of removing the salt from saltwater

Aircraft Carrier Strike Group

Aircraft carriers don't travel the open sea alone. They are accompanied by any number of ships, planes, and submarines to keep them safe. Together they are known as an aircraft carrier strike group.

11: number of aircraft carrier strike groups in the Navy as of 2013

100,000: pounds of weaponry carried on an aircraft carrier

CG Ticonderoga class (Cruisers):

guided-missile vessels that support an aircraft carrier

55 feet: width

567 feet: length

330: crew members

22: number in the Navy

DDG Arleigh Burke class (Destroyers):

guided-missile vessels that support an aircraft carrier in battle and in other missions

59 feet: width

505-509 feet: length

276: crew members

66: number in the Navy (including those under construction)

Littoral Ships (Independence variant):

built for speed and often used for near-shore missions

103.7 feet: width

419 feet: length

15 to 50: crew members

4: number in the Navy

Ballistic Missile Submarines (Ohio class):

provide underwater fire support for the aircraft carrier strike group

42 feet: width

560 feet: length

155: crew members

18: number in the Navy (including those under construction)

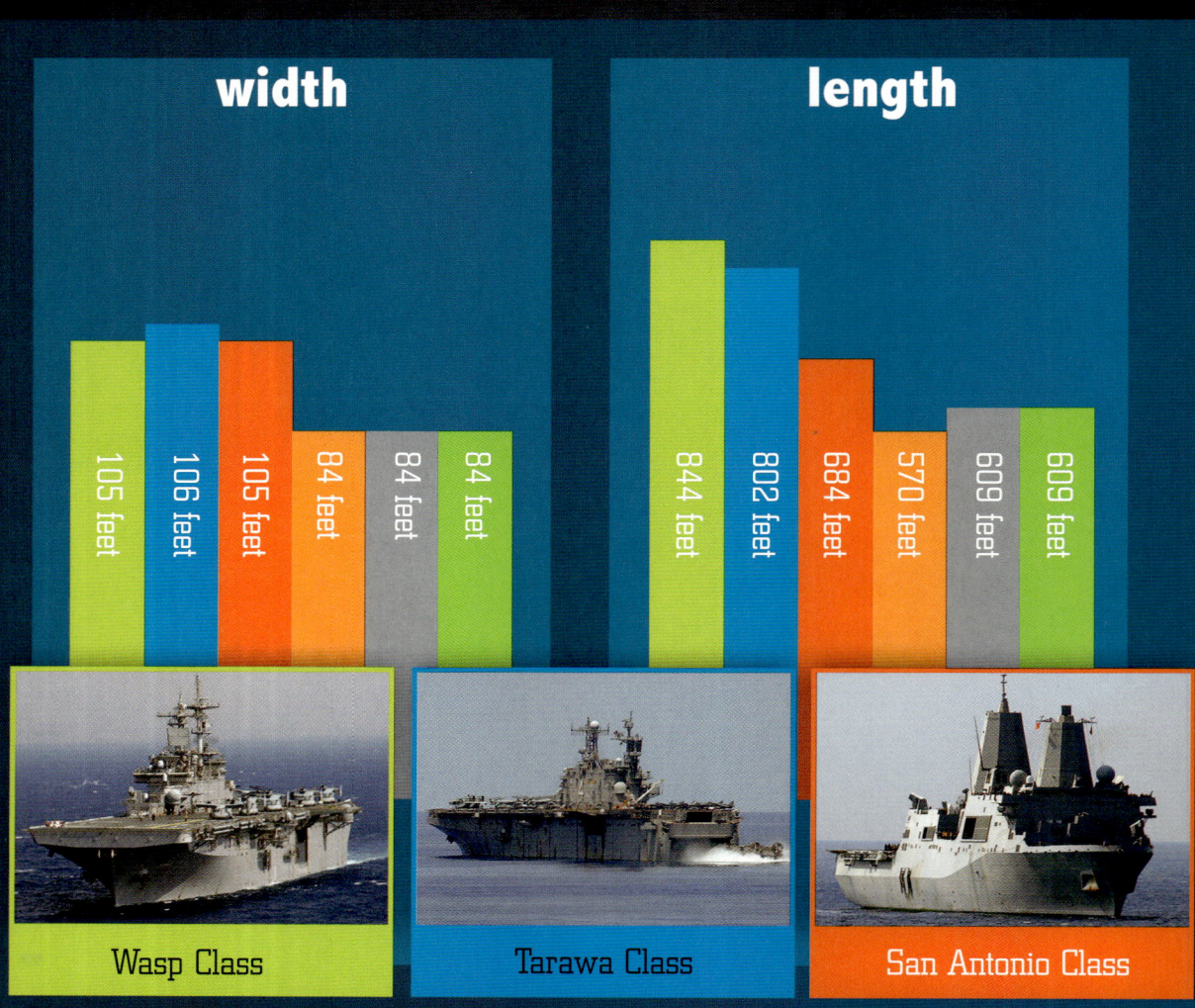

Amphibious vessels serve an important function in the U.S. Navy. They carry equipment, supplies, weapons, and sailors on the open sea. But they can also be used in land battles. The Navy uses different amphibious vessels for different missions.

speed
- about 20 knots
- about 24 knots
- about 22 knots
- about 21 knots
- about 20 knots
- about 20 knots

capacity
- 1,070 crew
- 964 crew
- 800 crew
- 900 crew
- 504 crew
- 504 crew

Austin Class | Harpers Ferry Class | Whidbey Island Class

Dock Landing Ships

transport air cushions for landing craft; provide docking and repair services for small ships, boats, and landing craft

Flying High in the U.S. Navy

While the primary Navy vehicles are ships, aircraft serve important functions in the Navy as well. Aircraft provide protection and warnings to ships and transport personnel and supplies. Aircraft also perform attack missions.

FA/18: used to attack ground targets, enemy ships, or other aircraft

565: FA/18s scheduled for delivery to the U.S. Navy by 2015

60.3 ft.: length

16 ft.: height

44.9 ft.: wingspan

1-2: crew members

flies at **50,000** ft. up to Mach **1.8+**

C-130 Hercules: hauls people and cargo for various missions

97 ft., **9** in.: length

38 ft., **3** in.: height

132 ft., **7** in.: wingspan

5: crew members (also carries 92 troop members)

E-2 Hawkeye: gives information to the carrier strike group, including weather conditions and battle plans

24-ft-wide **radar** rotodome: This equipment rotates and collects data to warn ships of danger and help in planning attacks. It can track 2,000 targets as far away as 342 miles. It also tracks weather.

360 degrees: radar coverage

5: crew members

57 ft., **6** in.: length
18 ft., **3** in.: height
80 ft., **7** in.: wingspan

Rotary Wing Aircraft (helicopters)

MH-60 Seahawk: The Seahawk family of helicopters has a combined 2.5 million flight hours in antisubmarine and surface warfare.

64 ft., **10** in.: length
18 ft.: height

3-4: crew members

wingspan—the distance between the tips of a pair of wings
Mach—a unit of measurement for speeds in relation to the speed of sound; Mach 2 is twice the speed of sound; the speed of sound is about 760 miles (1,223 kilometers) per hour at sea level
radar—an electronic device that uses radio waves to determine the location of an object, such as a flying airplane

Boot Camp!
Training Sailors

boot camp 8 weeks intense training at the Naval Recruit Training Command at Great Lakes, Illinois

To graduate from boot camp, every recruit must meet these requirements:

run
1.5 miles in:
- females: 16:20 minutes
- males: 13:40 minutes
- SEAL candidates (Navy special forces): 11 minutes

strength
- females: 16 push-ups and 46 sit-ups in 2 minutes
- males: 37 push-ups and 46 sit-ups in 2 minutes
- SEAL candidates: 42 push-ups and 50 sit-ups in 2 minutes and do 6 pull-ups

fire
an M-9 pistol and M-870 shotgun

jump
off a 10-foot tower into water below

swim
50 yards and spend 5 minutes in the prone position (dead man's float)

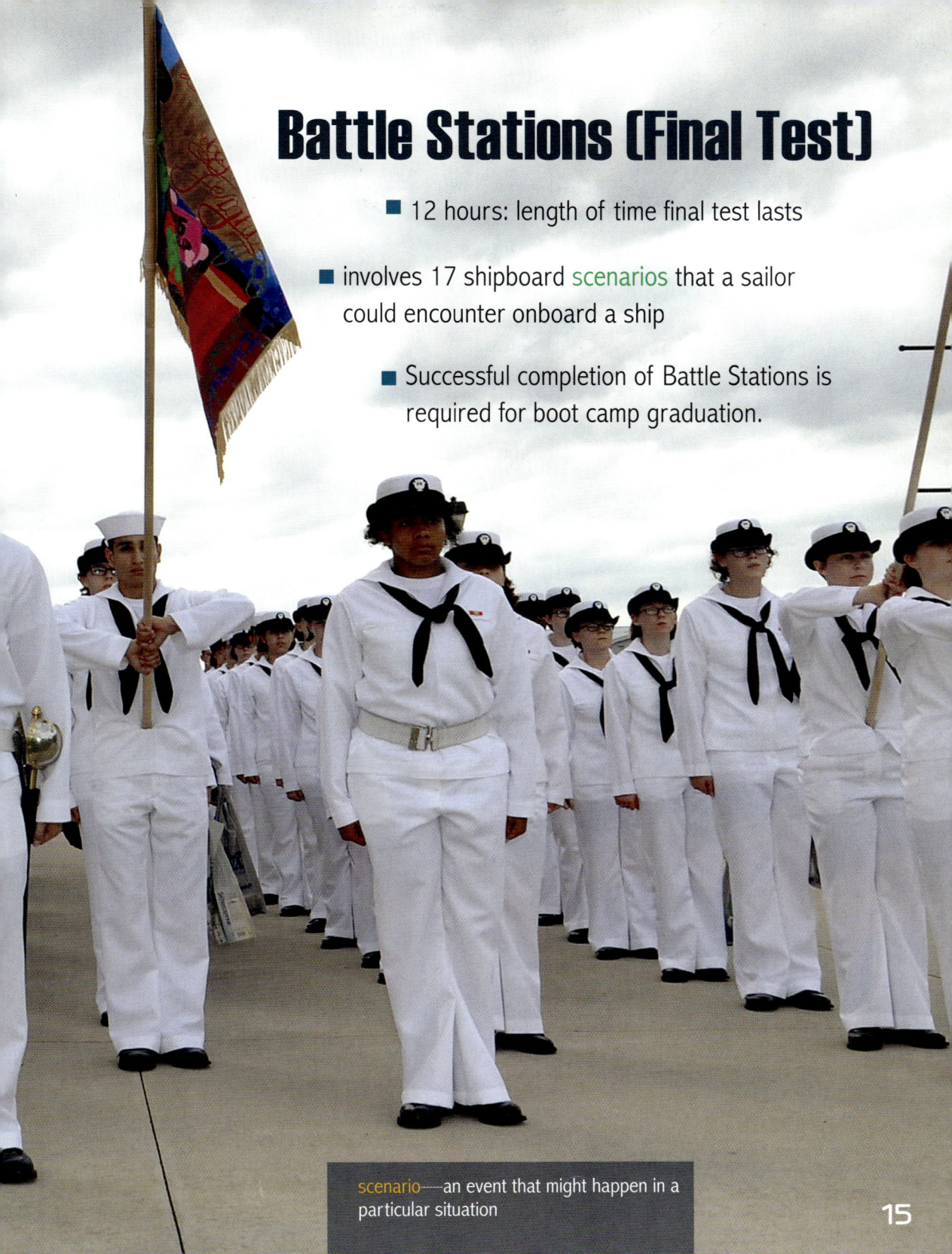

Battle Stations (Final Test)

- 12 hours: length of time final test lasts

- involves 17 shipboard scenarios that a sailor could encounter onboard a ship

- Successful completion of Battle Stations is required for boot camp graduation.

scenario—an event that might happen in a particular situation

Becoming a SEAL
SEa – Air – Land

The Navy SEALs are an elite fighting force that are part of the U.S. military's special operations forces. They are sent on some of the most dangerous missions imaginable. To become a Navy SEAL, a man must first join the Navy. Then he must pass the SEAL physical screening test. Finally, he has to complete highly advanced training, including Basic Underwater Demolition (BUDs) training, jump school, and SEAL Qualification Training (SQT).

Training includes:

running 200 miles

3 weeks of combat swimmer training

running **13** miles wearing 65 pounds of gear

26 weeks of SQT

5 days in a *simulation* as a captured POW

parachuting from 36,000 feet in jump school

28 days of cold weather mountaineering training

Every Year: About **2,500** Navy SEALs serve in the United States. On any day they can be deployed to 30 countries.

1,000
men start SEAL training every year

only **25%** of the men complete the training

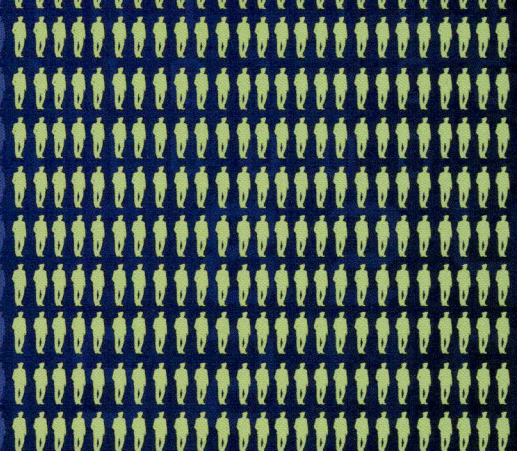

Upon completion of training, SEALs get a **$15,000** bonus.

- Only men are allowed to become Navy SEALs. This rule may change. The ban on women in combat roles was lifted in 2013.

simulation—an act that reproduces what would happen in reality

Life at Sea

Men and women in the U.S. Navy spend a large part of their time at sea. But sailors have very different experiences depending upon what type of vessel they sail on. Here's how life on board an aircraft carrier and a submarine compares.

Deployment

A submarine can be at sea up to 80 days before resurfacing.

Sailors on an aircraft carrier can be out to sea up to 9 months.

Workdays

Days on a submarine are 18 hours long instead of 24 hours. Crews work in rotating shifts: 6 hours on and 12 hours off

Depending on a sailor's job, he or she may work up to 22 hours in a day on an aircraft carrier.

Clothes

Sub crew members wear 1-piece blue overalls and sneakers. The overalls reduce the amount of clothing necessary on subs.

On an aircraft carrier flight deck, crews wear different colored shirts depending on their jobs.

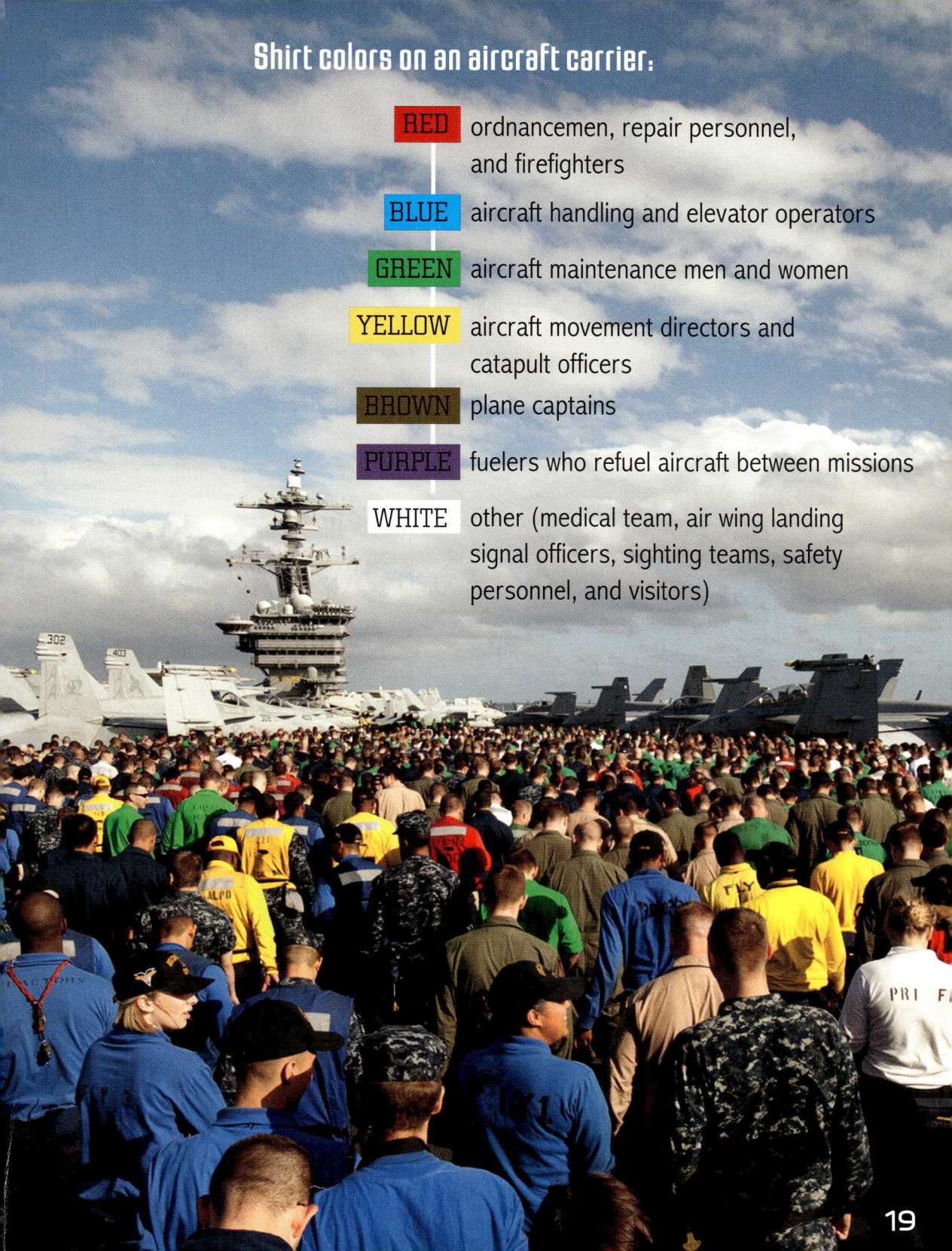

Shirt colors on an aircraft carrier:

- **RED** ordnancemen, repair personnel, and firefighters
- **BLUE** aircraft handling and elevator operators
- **GREEN** aircraft maintenance men and women
- **YELLOW** aircraft movement directors and catapult officers
- **BROWN** plane captains
- **PURPLE** fuelers who refuel aircraft between missions
- **WHITE** other (medical team, air wing landing signal officers, sighting teams, safety personnel, and visitors)

Into the Deep: Submarines

Hidden beneath ocean waves, submarines have always had an advantage over surface ships. Subs have improved dramatically since the first one was built. The first sub was called the Turtle Sub.

Turtle Sub

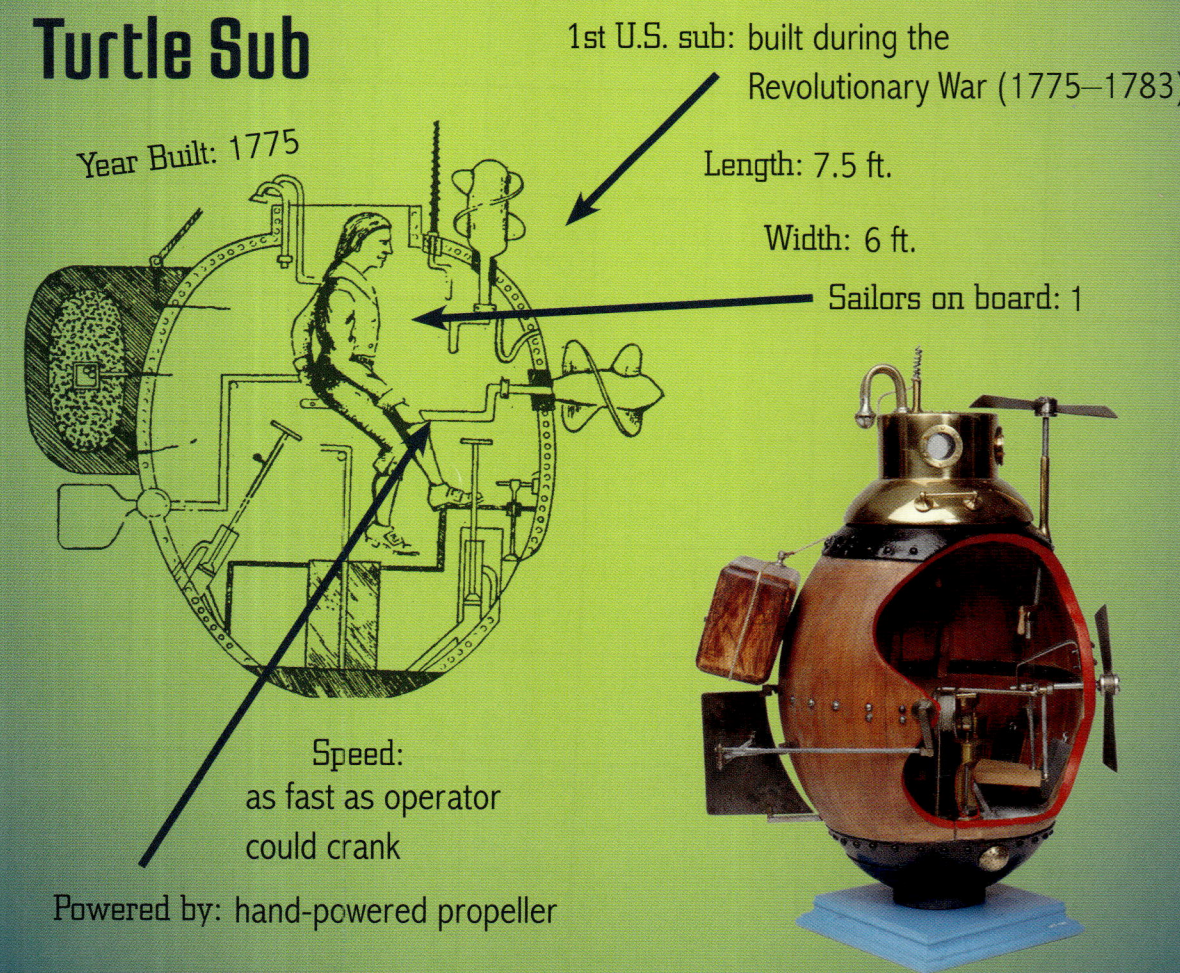

Year Built: 1775

1st U.S. sub: built during the Revolutionary War (1775–1783)

Length: 7.5 ft.

Width: 6 ft.

Sailors on board: 1

Speed: as fast as operator could crank

Powered by: hand-powered propeller

Weaponry: 1 mine torpedo loaded with 150 pounds of gunpowder

Fleet Ballistic Missile Subs, Ohio Class:

(also called "Boomers")
largest **nuclear** sub

- Year built: 1981 to present
- Powered by: nuclear power
- Length: 560 ft. (nearly as long as 2 football fields)
- Width: 30 ft. (3-story building)
- Weaponry: ballistic missiles and MK-48 torpedoes
- Sailors on board: 15 officers 140 enlisted sailors

nuclear—having to do with the energy created by splitting or combining atoms; nuclear reactors on subs use this energy as a power source; nuclear bombs use this energy to cause an explosion

Naval Weapons

Navy vessels require large, powerful weapons. The Tomahawk Cruise Missile and the MK-48 Heavyweight Torpedo are two long-range weapons.

Tomahawk Cruise Missile:

This long-range cruise missile can be launched from surface ships and submarines. It can carry one large warhead or a canister of small bombs. It is highly accurate and is mainly used for land attacks.

Length: 20 ft., 6 in.

Diameter: 20.4 in.

Wingspan: 8 ft., 9 in.

Weight: 2,900 lb.

Range: 1,554 miles

Speed: about 550 mph

First operational use: Operation Desert Storm, 1991

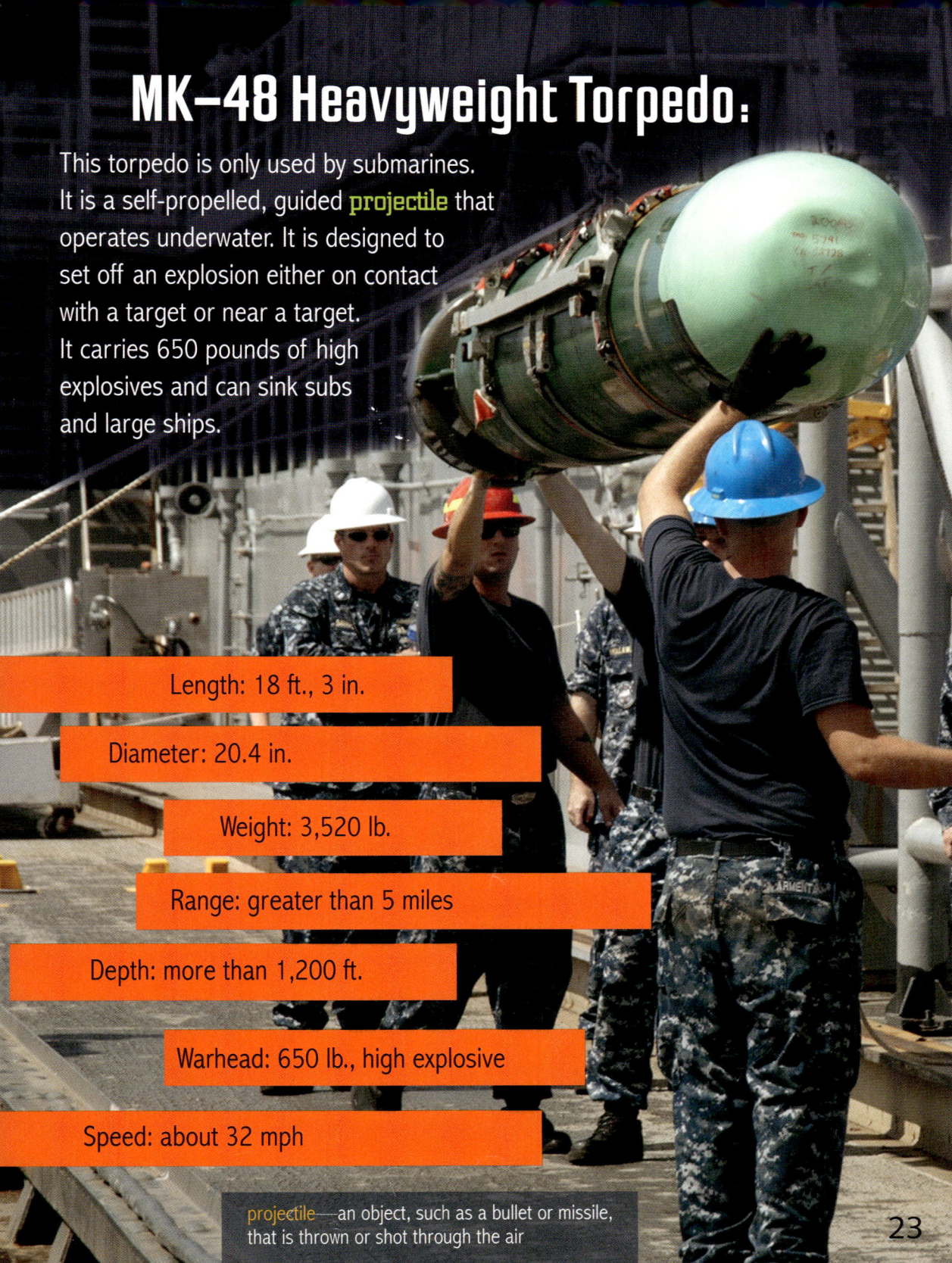

MK-48 Heavyweight Torpedo:

This torpedo is only used by submarines. It is a self-propelled, guided *projectile* that operates underwater. It is designed to set off an explosion either on contact with a target or near a target. It carries 650 pounds of high explosives and can sink subs and large ships.

Length: 18 ft., 3 in.

Diameter: 20.4 in.

Weight: 3,520 lb.

Range: greater than 5 miles

Depth: more than 1,200 ft.

Warhead: 650 lb., high explosive

Speed: about 32 mph

projectile—an object, such as a bullet or missile, that is thrown or shot through the air

Counting by

11	There are 11 fleet bands in the U.S. Navy. They are made up of professional musicians from around the country. They play in concerts, march in parades, and perform for leaders.
22	On December 22, 1775, the Continental Congress created the Continental Navy.
33	Code 33 is the department in the U.S. Navy that is responsible for developing warfare and energy technologies.
44	VA-44 Hornets operated as attackers and fighters during the Korean War (1950–1953).
55	Fifty-five women graduated from the U.S. Naval Academy in 1980, the first graduating class to include females.
66	During recruit training, a Navy SEAL can be away from home for up to 66 weeks.
77	The CVN 77 aircraft carrier was named after George H.W. Bush. He was the Navy's youngest World War II (1939–1945) pilot and the 41st president of the United States.
88	From 2001 to 2008, the Navy sponsored car number 88 in NASCAR's Nationwide series.
99	In 2009 the U.S. Navy saved $99 million dollars in fuel by decreasing how much energy each ship used.

Attack on Pearl Harbor

On December 7, 1941, Japan pulled the United States into World War II. The Japanese did this with a surprise attack on the U.S. Navy base at Pearl Harbor, Hawaii. They hoped to damage the U.S. Navy so badly that it couldn't fight back.

6:45 a.m. A U.S. ship spots a small Japanese submarine trying to enter Pearl Harbor. The ship fires on the sub and sinks it. U.S. forces do not realize this is part of a larger attack.

7:02 a.m. An Army radar station near Pearl Harbor gets a signal that a large group of planes is approaching. Radar technology is new, and technicians don't realize that the planes are Japanese.

7:55 a.m. The Japanese planes begin dropping bombs on Pearl Harbor and the surrounding areas.

8:10 a.m. A bomb blasts through the deck of the USS *Arizona*. It sets off more than 1 million pounds of gunpowder. The resulting explosion kills 1,177 men.

8:54 a.m. A second wave of Japanese planes joins the attack. This time U.S. troops are more prepared to fight back with anti-aircraft fire.

9:30 a.m. A bomb hits the USS *Shaw* and blows off the front end of the ship.

10:00 a.m. The attack ends.

United States | Japan

	United States	Japan
Ships sunk, beached, or damaged	21	at least 1
Aircraft destroyed or damaged	323	103
Personnel wounded	1,178	unknown
Personnel killed	2,378	64

Midway: A Decisive Battle

The World War II Battle of Midway is one of the most important battles in U.S. Navy history. The United States had three aircraft carriers based around the Pacific islands of Midway. The Japanese hoped to destroy those carriers. But U.S. dive bombers caught Japanese carriers refueling and rearming their planes. They attacked. Japanese losses were huge. This defeat of the Japanese eventually led to the Allied victory in World War II.

6 number of months after the attack on Pearl Harbor that the Battle of Midway took place

4 number of days the sea and air battle lasted—from June 4–7th, 1942

1 Japanese Naval Code: It consisted of more than 44,000 five-digit numbers.

U.S. intelligence cracked most of the code. Because of that, they knew the Japanese planned to attack Midway on June 4, 1942.

Losses
United States vs. Japan

United States
- 1 aircraft carrier
- 1 destroyer
- 150 aircraft
- 307 sailors

Japan
- 4 aircraft carriers
- 248 aircraft
- 1 heavy cruiser
- 4,800 sailors

Allies—a group of countries that fought together in World War II; some of the Allies were the United States, Canada, Great Britain, and France

Glossary

Allies (AL-lyz)—a group of countries that fought together in World War II; some of the Allies were the United States, Canada, Great Britain, and France

amphibious (am-FI-bee-uhs)—a vehicle or craft that can travel over land and also over or in water

base (BAYS)—an area run by the military where people serving in the military live and military supplies are stored

desalination (dee-say-lih-NAY-shuhn)—the process of removing the salt from saltwater

enlisted (en-LIS-tuhd)—describes a member of the military who is not an officer

fleet (FLEET)—a group of warships under one command

knot (NOT)—an international nautical unit of speed equal to 6,076 feet (1,853 meters) per hour

Mach (MAHK)—a unit of measurement for speeds in relation to the speed of sound; Mach 2 is twice the speed of sound; the speed of sound is about 760 miles (1,223 kilometers) per hour at sea level

nuclear (NYOO-klee-ur)—having to do with the energy created by splitting or combining atoms; nuclear reactors on subs use this energy as a power source; nuclear bombs use this energy to cause an explosion

projectile (pruh-JEK-tuhl)—an object, such as a bullet or missile, that is thrown or shot through the air

radar (RAY-dar)—an electronic device that uses radio waves to determine the location of an object such as a flying airplane

scenario (suh-NAIR-ee-oh)—events that might happen in a particular situation

simulation (sim-yuh-LAY-shuhn)—an act that reproduces what would happen in reality

vessel (VESS-uhl)—a boat or a ship

wingspan (WING-span)—the distance between the tips of a pair of wings when fully open

Read More

Greve, Tom. *U.S. Navy: Naval Power*. Freedom Forces. Vero Beach, Fla.: Rourke Pub. Group, 2013.

Llanas, Sheila Griffin. *Women of the U.S. Navy: Making Waves*. Women in the U.S. Armed Forces. Mankato, Minn.: Capstone Press, 2011.

Person, Stephen. *Navy SEAL Team Six in Action*. Special Ops. New York: Bearport Publishing, 2013.

Rudolph, Jessica. *Today's Navy Heroes*. Acts of Courage: Inside America's Military. New York: Bearport Publishing, 2012.

Internet Sites

FactHound offers a safe, fun way to find Internet sites related to this book. All of the sites on FactHound have been researched by our staff.

Here's all you do:

Visit www.facthound.com

Type in this code: 9781476539188

Check out projects, games and lots more at www.capstonekids.com

Index

aircraft, 12–13, 19, 26, 27, 29
   C-130 Hercules, 12
   E-2 Hawkeye, 13
   FA/18, 12
   MH-60 Seahawk, 13

Battle of Midway, 28–29
Battle Stations, 15
boot camp, 14–15

Operation Desert Storm, 22

Pearl Harbor, 26–27, 28

Revolutionary War, 20

SEALs, 14, 16–17, 25
ships, 5, 26, 27
   aircraft carriers, 5, 6, 8, 18, 19, 25, 29
   aircraft carrier strike group, 8
   amphibious vessels, 5, 10–11
   cruisers, 8
   destroyers, 9
   littoral ships, 9
   submarines, 5, 9, 18, 20, 23, 26

weapons, 8, 20, 21, 26
   MK-48 Heavyweight Torpedo, 23
   Tomahawk Cruise Missile, 22
World War II, 25, 26, 28, 29

Titles in this set:

- U.S. AIR FORCE by the Numbers
- U.S. MARINES by the Numbers
- U.S. ARMY by the Numbers
- U.S. NAVY by the Numbers